THE UGLY DUCKLING

Illustrated by Marge Opitz

Published by

THE TOON STUDIO™
OF BEVERLY HILLS

IT WAS SUMMER and lovely out in the country! In the midst of the sunshine lay an old farm surrounded by deep canals. Near the water a mother duck was sitting on her nest waiting for her ducklings to hatch.

One eggshell after another cracked open and little creatures stuck out their heads. But the biggest egg was still unbroken. When it did hatch, a large and ugly creature tumbled out.

"That is a terribly large Duckling !" said the
Mother Duck. "None of the others look like that
The next day the weather was fine. Mother Duck
came down to the water's edge with all her little
ones. Splash! into the water she jumped. "Quack!

Quack !" she called, and then one Duckling after
another tumbled in. The water closed over their
heads, but they came up in an instant, and floated
beautifully. The ugly gray Duckling swam about
with them.

"Quack ! Quack ! Come with me," said Mother
Duck. "I'll take you out into the world, and
introduce you to the duck yard."

But the other ducks in the yard looked at them, and said loudly, "Now we're to have all that crowd, too. There are enough of us already ! And look at that ugly Duckling. We won't stand for him !" And one duck flew up and bit him in the neck.

"Let him alone," said Mother Duck. "He does no harm to anyone. He is good-mannered and swims as well as any of you." But the poor Duckling that had been the last to hatch out and looked so ugly, was still being bitten and pushed around by the ducks.

He was in despair and decided to run away. H
went over the hedge fence, and made the little
birds in the bushes flutter up in fear. "That is
because I am so ugly !" he thought.
He kept running on, and came to the great
moor where the wild ducks lived. Here he lay
all night, weary and downcast. In the morning

the wild ducks flew up, and looked at their new companion.
"Pray, who are you?" they asked, and the Duckling turned in every direction and bowed as well as he could. "You are remarkably ugly!" said the wild ducks.

Again he ran away--traveling over field and
meadow, and floating down the waterways.
Toward evening the Duckling came to a little
hut, in which lived an old woman with her
Cat and her Hen. The strange Duckling was
noticed at once, and the Cat began to purr
and the Hen to cluck.

"Who is there?" called the woman, looking all around. She could not see well, and she thought the Duckling was a fat duck that had strayed. "This is a rare prize," she said. "Now I shall have duck eggs."

The Duckling remained at the hut. But after a time, when he failed to lay eggs, the old woman ignored him.

This made the Duckling feel sad. He thought of the canal and was seized with a longing to float on it. He left the hut and swam on the water and was happy, but not for long. Other ducks always slighted him because of his ugliness.

Then autumn came and the leaves in the wood turned yellow and brown. One evening, when the sun was setting, the Duckling saw a great flock of handsome birds. They were dazzling white, with long necks. They were swans. They uttered a peculiar cry, spread out their great wings, and flew away. They mounted so very high !

The Ugly Duckling had such a strange feeling as he watched them. He had never seen anything so beautiful. He turned round and round in the water like a wheel, stretched out his neck toward them, and uttered a strange, loud cry.

It would be too sad to mention all the misery
the Ugly Duckling had to go through during
the cold winter. He was so alone in the world!
He was lying out on the moor among the reeds
when the sun began to warm again and the
larks to sing. Beautiful spring had come.

All at once the Duckling raised his wings. They
flapped with much greater strenght than
before and bore him swiftly away. Before he
knew where he was, he found himself in a
lovely garden, where the fragrant lilacs bent

their long green branches down to the winding streams. From the thicket came three glorious white swans. They ruffled their feathers and swam lightly on the water. The Duckling knew the splendid creatures, and he was overcome by a strange sadness.

"I will fly to them, the royal birds, and they will kill me, because I, who am so ugly, dare approach them. But it is better to be killed by them than to suffer so much misery."
He flew into the water and swam toward the beautiful swans.

"Kill me!" said the poor creature, and he bowed his head toward the water, expecting nothing but death. But what did he see in the clear water? He saw his own image and he was no longer a clumsy bird. He, too, was a swan! The great swans swam round him and stroked him with their bills.

Some little children came into the garden. The youngest cried, "There is a new one !"
The other children shouted with joy, "Yes, a new swan has arrived ! And he is the most beautifull of all--so young and handsome!"
The new swan felt quite bashful, and hid his head under his wing, for he did not know what to think.

He was very happy, but not at all proud, for a good heart is never proud. He thought of how he had been scorned. And he heard the children saying that he was the most beauitful of all beautiful birds! Then he rustled his feathers, lifted his slender neck, and cried joyously,

"I never dreamt of such happiness when I was still the Ugly Duckling!"

THE END